The Language of Wildflowers

A collection of prose and poetry

Icy Belen Tumayao

Ukiyoto Publishing

Dedication

I dedicate this book to my father, Ignacio Tumayao Jr.. I wish you are now happy in heaven. Know that if there's a way for me to send a book there, I will. I love you tatay!

Acknowledgement

My greatest acknowledgement goes to God, the Father Almighty, for His unconditional love and for the gift of writing.

To my family, Cristeta (nanay), Jun Cris and Nash, thank you for your patience with all my tantrums.

My heartfelt gratitude also goes to Flordemae Tiwana, Rhea Mae Tagupa, Nona Grace Tuvalles and Nathalie Almario, for the amazing gift of friendship and love. Thank you for believing in me and for cheering me up when things don't go well. Thank you for the sturdy years of friendship, for the unforgettable sleepovers, for the countless bakasyon-grandes, for the beach parties and food trips we all enjoyed together. I really appreciate you all!

To my wonderful soul siblings, Jessica Pedrola De Ocampo, Christine Segumalian, Michael Andre Treyes and Anna Marie Sarroza, thank you for nourishing my soul and for painting my life with pastel colors. I still vividly remember the summer days we spent together as teens. Those memories are the highlights of my life. I appreciate all our conversations, all the laughter, grins, and tears we shared together. I wish you all the best in life and I really hope this book reaches you.

My sincerest 'thank you' to Dylan Timothy

Piper for being my muse and my confidant. When the world started eating my hopes away, you were there, empowering me to push through. I will forever treasure you for those wonderful gestures of saving.

To Carla Jane Subosa, Gladys Balibalos, Mary Wendel Amarillo, Shelalyn Falsis, Angelica Camino, Rhobylie Hadcan, and all my FGCI friends, thank you for the friendship, for the countless videoke parties, joy rides, and midnight galas.

I would also love to express my gratitude to Geneveve Tudence, Jessa Grace Jarce, Charina Torda, Raymund Jun Oberes, Sheenly Joy Torda, Aljohn Torreta, Jamille Kate Toong, Norvie Aine Pasia, KZ Genovea, and all my WISDOM batch '12 friends for always supporting my dreams and assisting me in my perennial struggles. You are all gems!

To Riezy Kate Gicaraya, John Mark Tagamtam, Marijune Malfarta, and all my Applied Math friends, thank you for the great years in the academe.

To Mariel Ledesma Terre, thank you for everything; for sharing the same passion and for helping me with all the publication prerequisites.

To Ruvina and Adam Graham, thank you for the heartwarming friendship despite it being online. You are like my siblings. And I can say that you two are the kindest, most loving souls out there. I'm so lucky to have met you!

To Logan Forster, thank you for the incredible friendship! It's amazing how we are so alike in many things. You inspire me to be a great writer! You are such a beautiful soul; you should know that!

To Rica Vie Llanillo, Cherrie Lyn Detablan, Eden Perez, Danah Jalandoon, Jemalyn Tavarra, Loren Andrade, Rency Tamon and all my LGU Tigbauan friends, thank you for the love and support.

To Daniel De Guzman, thank you for introducing me to Ukiyoto. You are a very great friend and a very talented writer. I really appreciate you!

To ninang Ofelia De Luna, thank you ninang for all the support.

My heartfelt gratitude also goes to the Ukiyoto Team for giving me the amazing opportunity to be a published poet.

And to all my family, relatives, and friends, this book will not exist without you. You all shaped me into who I am today.

CONTENTS

Prose

Skinny love

SHE WAS LOST, shuffling her feet along the endless pavement of a fading town. Her eyes were framed with moving pictures of haste- a crowd of strangers in their daily routine, dragging their dreams along with them. The sky above her head was a monochrome of gray, ready to burst into disoriented rains. It wasn't a beautiful scene. She sighed. She wasn't a beautiful scene either. She sighed more.

He was there, sipping coffee in a deserted coffee shop; taking pictures of empty tables out of boredom. The whole city resonated old acoustics, painting the atmosphere with the bluest of mementos. Outside the glass door was a deadbeat town bedaubed with colored drizzle and dark boots. It was a moving catastrophic painting, he thought.

Then, he saw her. A frame covered in sweatshirt and rugged jeans. Her curls bounced on her shoulders as she looked for anything that can shield her from the upcoming cloud burst. Footsteps were inaudible. The air was wet and mute. And then, in one moment of absentmindedness, her eyes met his.

The rain poured heavy on pavements and roofs. The smell of dust rose in all corners of the shop, mingling with the aroma of boiling espresso. Door chimes clang as strangers rush to find a comfy spot in the now-crowded cafe. Open umbrellas were all that was left outside. His eyes shifted from one face to another, hoping to find what he was looking for, but to no avail.

"Can I sit here?"

The voice sounded surreal that it took him seconds to react. When he did, a pair of hazelnut eyes was looking at him with bewilderment. His smile froze on his lips. He was unable to breathe for almost a minute, or so he thought. He nodded his head, questioning himself if it was an obvious nod or a shy bow. She took a seat across the table, carrying in one hand, an artsy saucer holding a smoking cup, and a thick old book in the other. They exchanged glances and shy smiles, learning how to react to a stranger who seemed to be more than that. Nevertheless, it was a moment to remember.

After the rain showers, one by one, the crowd dispersed into busy individuals catching up deadlines. Out of courtesy, she waved an enthusiastic goodbye. And the other did so. They parted ways, like what was expected of them. No exchange of names or random conversations, just seizing the moment up to the very last

And the world of romantics knew it was love... all people knew it was love, except them.

And if only they would meet again...

The night at carlton house

She was wrapped around the ethereal fingers of the moon, taming the night in its most splendid form. Flounces and tulle coated her in a delicate fashion, making the ladies of the Beau Ton shrink in envy. Her ringlets in pale gold bounced on her shoulders, a beautiful complement to a bejeweled tiara over her head.

She glided along the salon, joining the crowd of the peerage bedaubed with the finest quality of satin and laces; pearls and rubies, in all sizes. The Carlton House was filled with ladies in their pastel ball gowns, and overwhelming jewels, filling the floor with a touch of wealth and sophistication. The gentlemen were dressed significantly in their expensive tailcoats, pantaloons and kerseymeres, perfected with cravats and fitted white stockings matched with ebony-shaded shoes.

Chandeliers glowed like constellations, a metaphor of bountiful trees of diamonds pendent on the ceiling, outshining the candles seated on giant sconces. Under this brilliant crowd of lights, a quadrille moves in aestheticism, matching the rhythm of the stars.

She danced with a ravishing Englishman; whose eyes were the color of heavens- turquoise halos with a phenomenal luster, and whose facial features were sculpted by gilded angels. He was too beautiful- too breathtaking to be real. The warmth of his hand lingered on her palm like a breath of perfection meant to unfold that night.

Then, she woke with the clattering of charcoals in the grate, embers were floating like temporal fireflies, one by one, surrendering their bulbs to naught. She stood up in her worn-out gown, hurried to the fireplace, and sat at the hearth; her irises reflected the flickering remnants of fire, reminding her of her fantasy- unhealthy thoughts she brought with her in her dreams. Alas! It was a bittersweet fruit of her imaginings. Nothing more. It was long over, even before it begun.

She was forced to draw her consciousness back to reality. Her pale face and chapped lips worsen her dull room. Her hair, a bun of unruly strands was set atop her head in a no-fashion. Her thin hands were wrapped in a pair of greyed gloves- the only pair she got. She wasn't a looker, her lineage was known to be penniless.

She was a servant, carrying decanters to fill the goblets of proud noblemen, forever destined to watch carriages come and go, in every historical soiree possible. She dusted the furniture at Carlton House, done errands for a bunch of aristocrat, and of greatest service - a chaperone to the dowager. This is not a

Cinderella story, for fairytales never coexist with real-life tragedies.

Her ideal prince, a man of stature, was betrothed to a woman of grace. The perfect fit, of course; for all princes love princesses, not housemaids. And she, a servant, will continue to be... *just that.*

Withering with you

You came seven months ago, when I was crippled with responsibilities and negative emotions. I was a mess, crawling out of bed sleep-deprived and half-dead. I was constantly eating anxiety for breakfast, that got me starving and delirious, fragile and bleak. My soul was on a thinning process, and my nutshell was cracked. There were storms in the pockets of my cardigan, and dead flowers growing wild in my hair. I wasn't tamed. Not even by my own self...

Then you walked by me, a stranger in Urban Outfitters flashing your most dashing smile. I initially thought you were an idiot, probably lost. Maybe you'd ask for some directions which I couldn't give, because I too, was lost twice as much as you. But you took my hand as if I wanted a handshake. There were no giggles or butterflies back then. And I wasn't a poet. I remember I almost punch you but you dodged and laughed, and left me throwing rude stares at your back, mouthing 'the audacity' in the air. That was the beginning.

Days passed by as fast as a movie played at speed 2x. You were always there popping out of the blue, chasing my demons away, always loitering around to be noticed. I watched behind my glasses, overthinking about your motives. You were an open book, but written in French, with text printed in Palatino. I read your eyes wrong with false diction. *L'amour.* What a sad feeling to share with a stranger. I am never learning French.

Months later, you started acting like a best friend, prying at my life, digging my past like it's an active goldmine. I slowly accepted you like a souvenir from a wedding I don't want to be at. Then, I started writing poems. Maybe it was your smile that made me think of blooming metaphors and lush vignettes. I spent hours and more hours in a sad corner contemplating the curve of your lips, writing down your name on the footnotes like a bad habit. I was never a romantic. I don't know much about love. But if it happened to be a person, you would definitely share the same birthmarks.

Summer came; you held my cold hands and kept it warm, until a handful of asters started growing in my irises, pretending they were the best flowers that ever bloomed. And we gave them full credits. We stayed late at night watching the stars from different viewpoints. I learned about your scars, fears and melting points; the look on your face when you lie. I learned the gap between your sharp eyes and your soft heart; the dent on your soul caused by your past lovers. I embraced them all; the crest, the troughs, your high tendency to curse, everything.

But our love was fragile, and we had clumsy hands, a tragic combination. Now we are left breathing through cinders.

Love burned the walls we built around us, the same fire that burned our hearts to dust.

I know it's hopeless. But I'm hoping and hoping still.

Poetry

Shades of blue

i.

he documented everything;
the texture of sand between his toes,
the salty smell of the beach,
the foamy water with floating begonias,
the stray eyelash on her cheek
on that afternoon of April 29th.

it was a montage
of grays and blues,
a moving poetry
suspended in the air,
a patina of photographed smiles
from his old Polaroid.

ii.

he heard her chuckle
untangle itself
from the cluster of noises-
a song to his conscious state-
a faraway stimulus.

her windswept hair
smelled of magnolia,
of life unfurling
in pastel colors-
a swirl of fragrant art.

iii.

then there was silence-
loud and unforgiving.
a scratching sound
rose from the corner of his head,
like a static from a dying telephone.

he was alone after all,
mourning on a wrinkled handkerchief
and a parasol with her name.

tears sprung
like the raging sea
with the scent of nostalgia.

he lit one last cigarette
as he eyed the sky above,
searching for her face
in the cumulonimbus clouds.

the world halted midair.

running towards the shades of blue,
he was ready
to see her again.

Withering with you

your skin is a map
holding an endless
field of wildflowers
each with a name
and a story buried
within its roots.

i planted compass
roses in your eyes,
navigating in circles,
along the path of
dying stars you drew
with your fingertips.

i plucked the weeds
growing wild under
your lashes, tamed
the rain showers
flowing down your
cheeks, called it love

like i knew the word;
but seasons change,
temporal flowers die,
and all we are left with,
are blooming wounds
forever denied of healing.

The flower thief

her scent lingered
in the wind-

a kalachuchi skin-
plucked
and thrown away.

breaths forged
the trail of wildflowers,
a seamless art
tangled with the tendrils
of the setting sun.

he held her
longer than a lifetime,
watched the handpicked petals
wither slowly
in her eyes.

flat and brittle,

he kept her love
like a terracotta bookmark,

as she slipped

from the pages
of his heart.

Lumiere

words hang mid-air
coming from your lips,
untangling the strings of emotions
wrapping my chest
like a babushka doll.

l u m i e r e

my feet dance
to Tenerife Sea
matching a rhythm
i can't name.

your gaze
holds my windswept soul
steady,
my heart swells
like a waterfall
abundant with rain.

l u m i e r e

your ocean eyes
spill love;

a fervent pleasure
f l o w i n g
like raw molasses,
leaving a sublime trace
of wonder...

my lips
ache
to taste.

l u m i e r e

we stand close
a thin strand of air
separates our skin.
two bodies;
an analogy of pulsating breaths

meet halfway.

our hearts collide
like a beautiful disaster.

the victim,
we are yet to know.

Man of the wind

he taught me cartography;
the language of maps,
the texture of the Earth
against his index finger.

he's been to places,
cracked and dry.
left footprints on mountain slopes,
hillocks, and foggy highlands;
a stranger in the wild-
plotting stars,
dust to dust.

he mastered the shadows
on sundials,
rested on old farmhouses
with flaking walls.
he sailed seas and parted
rain like luminescent curtains-
a wholly citizen of the world.

he was a poet, with hands
harbored in a basin of ink,
cold and blistered.

he knew a lot of things-
from the crust to the sky-
but he doesn't know about love

and i can't teach him either.

The art of losing you

i stood there
f r e e z i n g
waiting for the sky
to drop sunflowers.

the howling wind
started to eat my soul away,
snowflakes descended in slow motion,
burying my footprints
like an act of treason.

my heart sank
at my feet
anchoring my soles
to the ground,
digging deep,
rooting for more pain,
scavenging for
a few more
jar of tears.

suddenly

i see endless
oceans framing

my eyes,
besetting me from
all sides;

i drowned.

my lungs
gave up like swollen balloons
bursting painfully.

my bones drifted
like broken oars
with little sense of direction.

I should curse love
for this kind of death.

but
why am i...
s m i l i n g?

The art of losing you… again

i spent time
repairing beating cardioids
like a profession;
graspers, needle holders,
and sternum spreaders
sat comfortably on a veneered table
living in the attic,
mimicking an exotic
surgical room.

the spiders on the cobwebs
watched how the stitches
were done, though none could patent
the way my hand weaves
the hollow of your chest,
and how the edges of your
broken skin
wrinkle beautifully
with every touch.

a mountain flower
stood dehydrated
on the window sill
sipping the last drop of rain
suspended in a styro cup

as old as your aging soul.

the trees undressed themselves
carefully just outside the door
like warm teenagers
feasting on the aftertaste of summer.

fall visited early this year,
though a bit too late
for the both of us.

i grew white hairs
watering that amaranthine flower
in your coffee cup;
fervently fixing a battered heart...

for someone else

to break.

Space drifter

he walked on the moon
barefooted, harvesting giant
succulents like spring flowers.

his eyes were plasma spheres
harboring stories of quasars
and vintage constellations
filling his canvas with
a draft of complex polygons
suspended in the sky.

i wrote poems about
his space suit and his
interstellar dreams
and he told me about
the shades of flaking clouds
and the flocks of lost
migratory birds-
with stories just like his.

i held him tight that night
as he drifted towards
the big dipper

never to be seen again.

Chasing goodbyes

our love was nothing
more than faded letters
kept in a drawer,
eating dust to survive.
we pretended it died
out of famine
as we discreetly moved on
free of guilt.

but...

i still have the scars
hidden under my sleeves
begging for attention
like a kid in the aisle
of a candy store
eyeing a bottle of gummy bears
and a pack of Reese's.

what is there to miss?

i don't even know
the curve of your smile
when you said a cryptic 'hi'
almost a month ago.

when you pulled me close-
but not too close
because you were afraid of love
more than losing it.

our hands
weren't made
to touch;
a depressed biology
of 'crown shyness'
moving from trees
to human fingertips.

and so
i planned to leave...

only to see
your addio note
sitting comfortably
on the breakfast table;
having a pep talk
with a cup of cold coffee,
and a stale egg omelette.

you won

in our race

to goodbye.

When you left

when you left,
nostalgia started breaking
silence in the room next door.
a cloud of soliloquy
broke the ceiling;
dust fell carelessly
imitating
a lame kind of rain.

i heard how lonely
the piano keys were
missing your touch
the way i do.
silence drove the walls crazy;
curtains hung mute
close to being suicidal.

a crowd of cacti
sat on the window sill
waiting for your shadow
to loom around.
a broken frame
holding our smiles
died from suffocation,
decaying on a trash bin

you forgot to trash.

we were
a variety of juxtapositions,
walking around love
with blind eyes.

i gave my heart too soon
and you proudly broke it twice.

Sometimes all we do is lie

your name is scattered
all over my brain
like a bad idea,
and you know
i'm lazy enough
to clean it all up.

i let you loiter around my headspace
like a VIP tourist
disturbing my thoughts
with your lopsided smile
and your broken
sense of humor.

you have this tendency
to be a tease;
working out on some lines
that fall short from your lips,
trying to make sense,
while your tongue
grasps the words
that assemble the sound
of jagged Poetry.

on cold days

you survey my heart
like a refugee searching
for a safer place.
you light a campfire
w i l d enough
to burn the walls
i put up myself,
find a couch
to rest your bones,
and label it
your territory.

almost poetic...

your lovely fingers
dissolve on motes of dust
and layers of ash
writing down
'I love you'
on the surface
of my soul.

~~~

you never really mean it...

but i'm still...

*I'm still smiling
at the thought.*
~~~

Homeless

we held hands
like amateur lovers
not knowing anything
about love.
we held hands
loosely,
with little intention
of keeping what we have.

flagrant.

you left my eyes broken
like leaky faucets
and you're the only
plumber i ever know.

helpless...

you ditched me
on the sidewalk
kicked me out
of your heart-
my rented space-
like a lousy tenant
who never paid the rent.

no notice.
no mercy.

the clouds
wept with me
as i dragged my baggage
of solitude
away from your door.

dripping sadness
filled my old boots
making it too
heavy for me
to move on.

i met my replacement
waiting on the curb
with an air
of confidence
and impatience,
she darted a pitiful look
at my shadow
which differed severely
from her shade.

(ah, the next tenant)

she passed me by
never looking back.

i lost my place.

my depressed bones
fold themselves
like old useless scaffolds
ready to be sent
in a dusty attic.

i was homeless
ever since.

Askew

when we met, the wind blew
in all the wrong places.
my heart was a disoriented tumbleweed
caught between the rails
of your picket-fence-bordered life,
stuck in discomfort,
seen but never found.

the day you took me in,
i withered in your palms
like a dehydrated crabgrass.
the diagnosis was mishandling.
but i stayed beside you
pretending to have dementia,
easing your guilt
with my weightless words.

i had loved you,
wide and deep
and with no sense of regret.
and you loved me too,
but a little wobbly.
the kind of love that will
surely fail a cross examination.

so we parted a year after.
when my heart
turned its back on me-
sick and delirious.
it grew tired of martyrdom
and of wearing a gown of caution tape
after a whole year lecture

on pain.

Blacklisted hearts

i.

you're a fraud
who elbows my heart like a bad habit
and im a first-rate fool
who gives you a weekly pamphlet
on how to break it well.

i don't know about love's agenda
but i have a patented bullet list
of the shitshows i must avoid-
only, i failed to
write down your name.

ii.

my heart has two legs
and a brain with topographical agnosia.
it walks on dangerous territories
without a first-aid kit,
or a single flare gun.

call it stupid
it won't even flinch.
that's how stupid it is.

iii.

so, when i met you,
I instantly fell- hard-
like a rookie rider
in a wild bull riding show.
i knew i needed surgery
but i went and let you treat me to dinner.

your love was a buffet table
and i was starving back then.
i licked the plates clean
without knowing a single bite
would cost me more
than a whole month meal
at Vikings.

and now
im staring at my bill
like a disgrace
wondering why i had to pay

-with my heart, upside down.

Wayside

i.

i met him five years ago
in his sweatshirt and levis,
a dog tag hanging around his neck.

he wrote about
Roman Gods and
underground madness,
while i obsessed myself
over artichoke petals
and potpourri pouches.

we went
to the same group of writers,
who eat poetry
for midnight snack.
i was the introvert
who sat near the trashbin,
beside the quiet redhead
named Taylor.

he was the brevity poet
who mastered the art of smiling
the one with a scar on the forehead
like a crescent moon.

ii.

our first handshake
took three seconds.
my toes curled like skimmed milk,
melting in my shoes.
it was a first-class flight to the clouds.
but i never told him
because he wouldn't understand.

our shadows grew
alongside each other
amongst the crowd
of tumbleweeds and
perennial wildflowers.

he colored my soul a bright tinge of rosa
and dusted my skin with his lips;
geraniums grew in his damp mouth,
portruding like art,
a masterpiece to say the least.

iii.

then, we talked
about marriage, and kids,
and where our first house
would grow roots.

years brew rains and tears.
everything ended in a storm
of mortgage loans and bills.

we pickled sunshine together
in countless jam bottles,
only to be emptied
at the end of every fight.

he changed,
or maybe i did.

love turned sour
like an old formaggio
spread on a moldy bread.

and up until now
my lips still wear
the aftertaste of regret.

The grave of lonely things

i.

he smelled of
rotten dreams and cigarettes,
oozing, sprawling,
coiling in the wind
like a twisted art.

and he told me,
he fell in love once
with a woman of art
he met at the train station.

he worshipped her name
like a biblical face, free of sins;

as she worshipped
someone else, wrote letters to
someone else, fell for
someone else, never that guy
who smelled of rotten dreams
and cigarettes.

ii.

i listened to the way

his broken tongue
dropped words loosely;
and for the first time
i heard how a heart
fragile and vulnerable
breaks in front of me
like classic chinaware
held by shaking hands.

iii.

last winter, the sadness-
thick as an avalanche-
got to him badly
a gunshot roared,
no one heard;
blood splatted
on the blue curtain
like an abstract painting
void of life.

his neighbors
found him 3 days after.
nobody missed him
the way
he should be missed.

one dead man, a lengthy poem,
and a dozen people in black

pretending they knew him
close enough
scattered on the cold tarmac
of the cemetery grounds.

nobody cried at his funeral
not even the girl
he worshipped like
a biblical face,
free of sins.

and that was how,

he chose to love.

Saudade

i.

i met you at a party
your hair, tousled, and
your shirt was wrinkled
like your forehead.

i was eating a fish pie
in a dark corner
watching the crowd
of drunk teenagers
yell about the ugliness of life.

you were drinking
for hours, and i was
there taking mental pictures
of the downside of humanity.

i walked home alone
and wondered if you got home safe.
or if the alcohol drove you
to a broken sidewalk.

ii.

months later,

we saw each other at
a local flower shop.
and i was relieved knowing
the booze hadn't killed you.

you forgot my name
and baptized me
the-girl-who-eats-fish-pies
though that was the first night
i got acquainted with that dish.

you left with a bouquet
of red stargazers
and a lopsided smile
that turned the familiar cobblestone path
into a Claude Monet garden.

. . .

years later,
i saw you walking down
the beverage aisle
of a withering grocery store,
i called your name
and you looked past me,

not remembering me anymore.

Uneven

when you left,
i started hugging walls
pretending they have
arms like yours.
my heart threw tantrums
noticing the difference.

but your shadow
is out of sight now,
probably waiting for love to show up
behind someone else's door.

while I'm here, drowning,
feeding on morphine,
reading my heart's repair manual

-which never worked before.

You love me like a shout out on april fool's day and i believe you

now, there's the wind
eavesdropping on the glass door,
murmuring silence.
but there's nothing here anymore.
i fed our conversations
to the dogs.
just the way you like it.

i buried a pile
of false hopes yesterday
and made a mental note
not to dig it up (again)
tomorrow morning.

but your smile
is a traitor
handing me a shovel,

and guess what?

i'm still digging here...

The tragedy of us

there i was
covered by an avalanche
of nostalgia
spilling from the loose pockets
of raging winter
(coming from your lies.)

tears sprung
like tiny broken things,
an analogy of pain
whispering softly:

"oh love doesn't hurt you.
people do"

my teeth
clattered in dissonance,
my soul shivered
underneath my skin.

the broken
flowers you gave me
surrendered all their colors
to yesterday,
wearily breathing out

sepia memories
into the cold, cold wind.
i froze,
somewhere
deep inside your eyes,

hoping,

waiting,

yearning,

until you learned
to shake me
off your lashes

for good.

you found love

the very same moment

i lost mine.

Letting go

this solitary madness
sits with me in the corner
and teases me to let you go.

i feel old and broken.
my bones are dead inside.
my mouth-
too lazy to yawn.

i have a separation anxiety
with all the forgotten
Christmas trees of the world.
my eyes grow tears
and they are always thirsty.
the kind of garden i would never have.

these metaphors.

while the sky
blushes with pyroclastic wonders,
my heart melts
waiting for a sign,
as i sort out
your name
from all the words

clustering within my soul.

my lashes play dumb
as i comb the desperation
out of my hair
2020 is the year for me to heal
so

i need

to let

you go.

Invisible

let us speak
of flowers and poetry
of books half unread
left on quiet nooks.

let us read
the post-its pinned
on aging corkboards
captioning old photographs
in a wallflower's room.

let us sing
the lyrics scribbled by gentle hearts
on brittle pages
of countless sentimental notebooks.

let us take pictures
of the moving clouds
or the heart-shaped creamer
sprawling on our coffee.

stop for a while
and let us notice
what we kept missing
all along...

for once
(forget about singularities)

let us notice...

us.

Untitled

~ my heart
    is a local diner
  with a broken signage
    and a deserted parking lot.

it sits along
    a parched highway
  where rainclouds
    are a myth,
and tumbleweeds
    outnumber people.

it has been empty
    for one score and five years,
mourning over
        its peeling walls,
  nursing its own
        dusty countertop,
  while the perennial termites
    feast on its aging pillars.

it has nothing to offer
    just old cheap wines
  and burnt steak
    so it's not a wonder

why no one ever stayed.

July blues

my room talks to me
in a language
nobody understands.

there is so much
sadness here
resonating from the walls,
springing from the floor
like old abandoned flowers.

it seeps through the window
navigating the cracks-
wickedly,
like the savage,
unending, July rain.
i am floating
on a makeshift
bed of anxiety.
my body-
a giant tear bag
wrapped in human skin.

my eyes falter
like dying candles

my heart,
a pincushion of sin.

Pitch black

some days,
his bones are quiet
nursing a chapbook
of poetry
for the disoriented world.

his limbs
        fold,
            unfold,
like a skeleton tree with
tiny broken branches,
        dancing
    with a bleeding quill.

at night, he keeps an archive
of ragged people
and bruised sunsets
as his deformed heart
slowly drowns in a sea of booze

filling his ribcage to the brim
heaving,

        bleeding,

wondering,

how many bluebirds
            are there

left to drown.

Deep indigo

in that crowded place,
i casted my hopes

and worries in the air.
i was ready to let go
of all my tearbags

when

i saw you
with your sad eyes.
your footsteps
exuded a series of poetic impulses
the crowd never heard before.

you were a shade of rain, partly,
or a phase of drizzle personified.

the crowd shuffled between us;
a movement of monochrome blues,
staining the homeless wind.

the collage of faces
painted a hollow sky
and a bleak, receding ocean.

we were all blue.
i knew.

but what shade of blue are you?

Unsent

the houseplants
in my room withered
from lack of care.
and i wanted to apologize
in a language
they would understand, but
i couldn't find the words.

so i invited a couple of stray cats
to grieve with me
for days.
they licked their paws
after eating
a plate of fish bones,
settled on a rug
and purred.

i've been calling it therapy
for a year now.
my mother
was completely oblivious of the
dying houseplants, stray cats
and dead butterflies
decaying
in the pit of my stomach.

motes of dust grew thick
on the piano keys, and the
coffee table book, and the hemlines
of a skewed-hanging curtain
i find impossible to fix, until now

my heart has been a home
of dust bunnies
and fragile mementos,
with the yard,
a safe ground
for lonely tumbleweeds
who don't complain
about loneliness.

my mother will never know.

Starry night

my sad eyes welcome
the words of Sylvia Plath
suspended on a strangers'
chapped lips,
Lady Lazarus
'she sobbed'.

a faint echo
bounces off the walls
a repetition,
of black and white mementos.
life is running dry, impatient
d r o o p i n g
like withered sunflowers.

i keep my tears
in a bottle,
thinking about Bukowski.
my grave waits patiently
for my skin and bones
to lose the battle
~am i blue enough?

my thin fingers
trace the stars

drawn by Van Gogh
on a sky canvas
as I converse
with the shadows
leaning against the wall.

Everything's okay until it's not

i sink here,
unadorned,
until some wandering fruit flies
found me peeling
my flesh, looking like
an overripe peach
stranded on top
of a month-old trash.

i can't give myself a name
or a decent definition.
i am sort of a pending hiatus
blowing dead butterflies
in the circulating air
creating a circus
in my head,
with a less funny clown
and a black canvas tent.

my soul is broken
like a marionette
smashed on a brick wall,
like a cheap jar
knocked down
by a whimpy kid,
like a poet eaten

by months of insomnia,
and aneurysm
being a constant threat.

(you're my therapy
but you're tired of me
i guess)

i scatter my tears
like a hobby
hoping they would
grow into wildflowers
but the irises in my eyes
are all dead now.

...and it's obvious
that you don't give a damn
anymore.

Bruised hearts die young

rusted utensils
started digging
on an empty plate,
creating
a fraudulent sound
of a happy meal.

her stomach lurched
screaming twofold
in between chapped lips.

her bruised soul
murmured a complain
but all ears were dumb
to understand a thing.

dilapidated eyes
wandered towards the ceiling
where
the ghost of yesteryears
collected a million sighs
in the form
of dust.

she swallowed the pain

of being less
than anyone.
reality grabbed her by the throat

as the crowd
preached
on her birthrights...

as if
they knew the word.

Meltdown

. . .

and we die
along with monarch butterflies,
and stray cats,
and dotted orchids
growing in your uncle's yard.

we die,
looking at each other
unabashed
as people
pass us by
like dejected clowns.

we die every day
on countless train rides
commuting on the edge
of our open graves,
humming a playlist
of familiar requiems.

we die
with pages and pages
of unpublished poems,
purchased tickets,
and a set of faded receipts;
rotting altogether in our dirty pockets,
waiting for salvation...

or none at all.

we smell of
formaldehyde,
sweat and lavender,
a perfume too strong
for the crowd.

we die
breathing;
staring at death
eye to eye,

never blinking,
and
never afraid.

Dark and darker shades

broken terminals hold a camp of souls
drowning in a flood of morning coffee,
staring coldly at week-old newspapers.

cigarette butts spill on reeking trash bins.
a railroad runs across the deadbeat town
as shades of blue fill and empty the seats.

sad eyes wander on broken suburban-
a gray scale panorama of faint smiles.
the sunrise, a lifetime away from here.

Same old shadows

same old shadows
loiter in the parking lot
cursing the world
for the way it is.

same wasted youth
carrying empty bottles
waging wars
against the midnight wind.

and they breathe
and they scream
but nobody hears
they call it freedom
but it's all bottled-up fears.

and Jack's talking to the streetlights,
looking up above
saying life was a thief
and that he was robbed.

his friend was retching on the sidewalk
dead dreams spilling from his eyes
the city faded in the background
along with all the neon lights.

and they breathe
and they scream
but nobody hears
they call it freedom
but it's all bottled-up fears.

I will leave this here to rot

most days
i dont know how to be useful
so i sleep away
dreaming of Bukowski,
hoping he would hand me a drink
and a book, that would fit my pocket.

maybe we'd talk about
the suburban
and the numerous broken people,
with all their broken things;
grieving inside cheap motel rooms,
sinking on old mattresses
that nursed a generation of souls.

i will listen
to each slur
that unveils every tragedy
of human imperfections
clinging on to cold bottlenecks
with limited lifelines,
counting analogies
of gray scale rainbows
and scattered rains.

blue is our color
we see it in the shadow
of a stranger walking out of Walmart
empty-handed,
in the eyes of a bartender
handing mojito to a
maudlin customer at 2am,
in the quiet hallways
and auditoriums
ghosted by drunk poets.

"there is a loneliness
in this world so great"

that it spills
like a cask of Ale emptied
in a single pint mug,
and nobody cares
because each one has a cask
and a box of unlit cigarettes
left to waste.

there are empty cans
along the street to kick
all the way home.

i wonder
when i will be sober.

Paper girl

She paints her sorrows
with metaphors and word collages-
Each stroke spells her heartbreaks well.
And her eyes are floodgates
with tears free-falling...
Drenching her soul's weak outer shell.

Shards of broken clouds split the skies;
Cloudburst is dressed in crimson hue,
Gray hearts are cold, silent and smug,
All rainbows fade to shades of blue.

Purple art sprawl on her skin;
This paper girl keeps painting still...
And every touch from her vintage brush,
Leaves deep wounds that would never heal.

She's everything creased and crumpled-
A flat canvas embossed with scars.
Her soul is pale- a torn sheet trampled.
Her life, a chain of dying hours.

And when she thought love could save her,
It just tore her into feeble shreds.
Her heart was burned in dinner date candles-

Windswept trails of ashes spread.

Lifetime wounds grace her pallid flesh,
As ice cold tears continue to spill
She's an artist of bruised tragedies
And this paper girl keeps painting still...

Void

i am suspended
somewhere between the stars
floating in a space continuum
unknown yet to man.

i sink on gases
of purple and blue
expanding and shrinking
in zero dimension.

my irises falter

my soul, warped

the void
consumes me
from the inside.

save me
please

before
I'm
gon-

Keeper

she ventured
broken terminals
barefooted.

her little hands
collected shadows-
cold and blue.

she carefully
placed them
on a parchment paper,
side by side,
like raw words
escaping from a poet's tongue.

her palms
patted the sobbing darkness
and wiped the tears
out of the page.

she was a keeper.
of the lost,
the broken,
the insignificant,
the abused,

the forgotten.

she was a keeper
of every misfit
who ever cried for help.

she was a keeper
who forgot to be

a keeper to herself.

Un fiore giallo

she was just a speck of earth-
a careful girl
in a sea of careless people;
musing back and forth,
with broken flowers at her feet.

she mumbled obsolete rhymes
and whispered sonnets to the wind

the lyrics faded,
the air was mute,

the entire world became her nook.

Giardiniere

he was an empty shell
with his heart hanging askew
underneath his worn out sweatshirt
and scarred skin.

he bartered love for nothing
gave up songs for none
wrote poetry for a broken girl,
who's in love with a broken man.

To a poet

Your eyes hold a promise
of a thousand vignettes;
a sewn art of narratives
and sunshine metaphors.

The soft wind in your hair
is unborn poetry
carrying a hefty cloud
of sonnets and cinquains
figuratively crafted
with a wreath of sweetbay magnolia.

Your heart is brevity;
a tapestry of haiku and senryu,
decoupage of ballads
in a sea of poetic musings.

You are made of rhythmic quatrains-
an endless ocean of poetry.
And i'm an anthophile
with lungs made from flowers

forever drowning in your smile.

The face of summer

we chase skip beats
on countless road trips;
freewheeling
under the bluest sky
where
the tendrils of the sun
float in the wind
like second skin.

we smell of
mayflowers and freedom
two souls,
s e a b o u n d e d,
in love with each other
in a poetic way,
beyond sunlight
and spring
put together.

your eyes hold euphoria;
a moving art,
a frame of a million flowers,
an indie song-
soft and lasting-
there is too much in it
i could not name
too much of something...

b e a u t i f u l.

now,

let us keep
the acoustics close,
windows down,
humming to 'The Paper Kites',
sighing at sepia memories
we pass by.

smiling candidly~
we stash sunset memories
t o g e t h e r;

my arms wide open,
hugging the nostalgia
thick in the wind;

dreaming of more sunflowers,

   more laughter,

      more Vance Joy,

         more skip beats,

with you.

Beautiful strangers

to you...

your heart beats
in metaphoric assonance-
a beautiful,
impeccable kind of rhythm.
you are laced with ink pens
and abstract word puzzles
compounding everything
about recognizable aestheticism.

your mind is a maze
of riddles and myths,
anecdotes and poetry,
polychromic butterflies,
altogether crafted
under the weight
of your laurel crown.

you own the stars and the constellations,
the seas and the winds,
the wildflowers and the moving clouds,
the curvature of the horizon,
and beyond...

and I don't know

if you know
that you are one BEAUTIFUL SOUL
coated in human skin.
your quill tells stories
the most profound
and intelligent
every pair of ears should hear.

you are a BEAUTIFUL STRANGER.
a Poet.
a Wanderer.

let us all head home.
(let me go home with you...)

Hushed love

to the guy with muted lips--

you eat words,
crush them with your teeth,
'til the syllables
break down
into meaningless letters-
a crowd of singularities
bouncing on your tongue...
altogether,
filling the corridors
of your throat--

just crowding there.

and when you part your lips,
words sink inside you
like residues
atop deadbeat decibels.

your emotions
act like rusty crowbars,
digging what's left of the mess.

my love,
I wonder how you sound.
but it will never make me...

love you less.

Tie me to the stars

one day, the world
will grow wings.
it will perch on a cosmic tree
devoid of hate,
hardships and pain.

people of all color
will smile at the sky,
at the vastness
of our Savior's grace,
at the beauty of
infinite life ahead.

we'll smell the flowers
growing on our palms.
we'll praise the sun,
we'll tame the rain,
we'll let the wind
carry our woes away.

we will be filled with
absolute gladness.
the one that will soften
the untamed hearts.
we'll love ourselves more,

our countless flaws,
and all our broken counterparts.
oh, tie me to the stars!

where our thirst for happiness
will finally be quenched.
our poems, recited.
our dreams, hailed.

i will wait for that day
to come.

we will wait

t o g e t h e r.

The birthrights of a dead poem

i think i have swallowed
a broken hummingbird
in my sleep. and it died right
in the middle of my lungs.

a rose garden started growing
in the pockets of its wings-
blooming like art- coiling around
my fragile spine.

a rare shade of indigo
spilled in my blood-
sprawling in my veins
like a sea of dead ink.

my tangled breaths
escaped the trenches of my throat;
merciless, shell-shocked,
armed with nothing but quills.

. . .

there is so much sadness
in between dislocated smiles;

bruising lips just by
spitting out   --poetry.

For poetry

you are a papier-mâché
with distorted silhouette,
dancing along
the crowd of broken marionettes...
stitching the edges
of this wrinkled world
like never-to-fit puzzles.

button eyes,
fake laurel crown,
creased skin,
crumpled rug cling
to your limp shoulders
coating your flaws.
you're a breathing doll
made of pulped paper.
nothing else.

but you unravel
the faults on the crust,
scrutinize helium,
recount sky snow balls
over your head.

while all broken things

laugh and mock...
you come around
to fix them.

for what?

your chapped lips
whisper...

for *POETRY*.

On writing

when i have time
i get away.

i elope
with all my muses
carrying poetry
in both our pockets
and duffel bags.

i fly
to a place
where my heart
could be a full grown flower;
where the wind is heavy
with colors of spring.

i tiptoe
over lotus dreams
and embrace
my lucid imaginings
the way i
embrace you.

when i have time
i escape

the suburban
of rotten routines,
the dark alleys
with loitering
dead dreams.

i walk on
till midnight

i run through
the dawn

and in the morning,
i know,

i know
i will be home.

Poetry people

we writhe on a puddle of ink
harboring our bones
till we become
breathing quills.

we walk on parchment paper
and leave footprints
in metaphors.

we hide between line breaks
and after ellipsis-
casting our shadows
in written words.

we lie on pages,
pressed against each other;
skin touching
paving way
to a beautiful friction...

and then,
we part.

u n b o u n d e d.

eyes trace our curvatures,
lips turn our souls
to decibels.
we leap from paper,
wander nowhere, lost
and never found.

we are POETRY
pretending
to be POETS.

(or the other way around.)

Rain

poetry slipped
from the grip of the clouds

u n r e h e a r s e d.

words fell like rain
scattering on pavements,
filling potholes
with raw metaphors
in the shade of asphalt.

the windswept rhymes
fogged up the window
of a drenched town.
free verse was seen
riding on the back of the wind,
bare and cold.

d a z z l e d

a line
from a couplet
got tangled
in your hair
like a broken

peineta.

your palm
caught a stray drop
of brevity
heavy like an ode

and

while all other eyes
see only

r a i n

you see a cloudburst
of words.

Behind poetry

when I look at Poetry
I don't see just words...

I see an artist
frowning at the crimson sky
trying to detain
the antiquity of sunset
in his verses.

I see a girl
painting her walls black
hiding her fears
in hoodies and crafted metaphors
(besmearing the mirror to hide the beast).

I see a torn lover
stitching his heart with a pen;
clustering a bouquet of broken flowers
for an ode never read.

I see a child missing home
humming his mother's lullaby.

I see a drunk teenager
trying to figure out life.

I see an old man
waving his last goodbye.

I see shades of pain
sometimes,
faces of euphoria.

when I look at Poetry,
I don't see just words.

I see People...

I see YOU.

Moonchild

in the heart of
the tinted rainforest,
his name was carved
on a century-old boulder;
a hundred aspen trees
were the scaffold of his home.

he drank the mountain clouds
under the vast shifting heavens,
where his footprints once marked
his long-forgotten throne.

the indigo shadows
wrapped the hemlines of the wind,
rising through the thickly-veiled smoke.
the whirlpools in his eyes
held a living curse,
of how his heart
was bound to be disowned.

the fallen moonchild
wandered for years,
a myth he was to some.
but his name still
echoes in the woods,
a familiar face...

forever gone.

Crypt king

he grew in an orchard
of sins, flourished alongside
perennial thorns and
sharp, twisted weeds;
curses and thunderclaps
were his lifelong lullabies.

his throne was a shrine of thistles
with roots growing from
decaying catacombs,
buried in the mist of time,
hiding the contorted silhouettes
of aging, underground shadows.

in the penumbra of the night
he rose, with a crown made
from brittle twigs and bones-
the gunmetal moon
morphed into light,
spilling on his wicked, abstract smile.

Mr. Straitjacket

he wore the color of solitude-
with his gory skin
a straitjacket for his soul.

i saw the unfathomable
abyss in his marble eyes,
the intensity of chaos
and the narrative of pain,
housing a game
for morbid onlookers.

he held my gaze tight
like a predator to a prey,
breathing heavily through
corrupted repo lungs.
a lost nyctophile
licking the edge of darkness,
tasting the freedom of
cold and warm breaths alike.

his intentions
were clearly sinful

i knew from the very start.

but i let his wicked smile
devour me...
a catapult
straight to the heart.

Wolfboy

he smelled of petrichor
and damp woods-
the gray perfume of weeping clouds
tangled in the breeze,
coating the leaves
exhaled by giant cedars.

his doleful cry
wrapped the windswept trees
in a gothic fashion,
painting shivers
down the spine
of a thick forest fog.

the alabaster moon
hailed his song
like a century of haunting nocturnes
creeping on brittle branches
as he freed himself
from the purple rain.

burning eyes
lit the pitch black darkness,
embers faded,

as the shadow of a boy
rose before
his pack of timber wolves.

My heart is a graveyard of dead stars

the suburban
and aging fields
wrap the globe,
a ball hanging
alongside
celestial snowflakes
where the mixed tape
of angels can be heard.

loose hands
juggle a thousand spheres
orbits tangle
like iridescent strings
weaving a palpable
cosmic art;
leaving traces
of interstellar clouds
on dangling fingertips.

stars rub wrists
embers light the
pitch black darkness
with a burst of neon dust...
sprawling on
empty spaces,

coiling on planetary rings,
slowly eating the remains
of aesthetic supernovas.

the Universe
sits still
pregnant with
quasars and nebulas,
galaxies sleep in its
womb,

c o m p l a c e n t.

a billion
greyed souls
weep in harmony

curling into a ball
like a crowd of pangolins
unheard,

unseen,

unfelt,

bartering a lifetime
of breaths
for a poem.

Female's tears

you squeeze my bones
and rip my flesh

words drip
from the cuts on my skin
shattering on the tile floor-
broken-
like fragments of some
dusty chinaware
left unfixed.

your kisses are snakebites
creating bruises on my skin;
hissing in silence,
the savage languages
of flaws
and human atrocities.

your hands are
a noose around my neck;
their prints,
a lifetime necklace-
an ugly ornament
made from sin.

my body,
a battlefield
of wounds and scars-
a wrecked art
you pronounced
as your wholly masterpiece.

but

I am not
your own handiwork.
I am a woman.
I breathe and love as a woman.
I am made of delicate things,
warm and fragile, both.
skirts and heels,
don't comprise me.
I am far more than that.
and I tell you...
you do not own my soul,
not a piece of it.

I am a woman.
I am not your own handiwork.

though my tears
never get to your eyes...

I AM A WOMAN.

I AM A WOMAN.

I AM A WOMAN.
so please...

treat me
and honor me
as one.

Primavera

Primavera,
you carry on your skin
the fragrance of spring,
weaving onto
the astral fabric of your dress;
leaving traces of speckled flowers-
like scattered potpourri
meant to breathe perfumes.

Primavera,
the sweetest buds
hail your name
in glorious successions.
You float splendidly
on nature's alleyways
freshening up
the faces of withered flowers.
Je ne sais quoi!
Such magic your fingertips hold!

Primavera,
you paint the trellises
with burning orange and bottle green-
a garden decoupage
set to sprawl on arcadia-

slowly eating away
the canvas of earthly colors.
Vines cling on your curves,
foliage grow on your hair,
and your dear eyes
are loopholes to empyreal wonders!

Primavera,
you hold pure aesthetics
in primal degree.
Kingdoms fold at your feet,
generations of souls
write you poetry,
and every blossom,
everywhere,
speaks on your behalf.
(I hear them singing!)

Primavera
the Allegory of Spring,
you are freed art,
a nymph,
a masterpiece
birthed from perfected strokes
of an artist
who will live on...

as long as you do.

Autumn

the trees
bare of leaves
weep
for a seasonal demise.

the windswept branches
sway to
a mute lullaby
floating
through the breeze.

the coldness howls
echoing through
alabaster pavements
swirling piles
of broken shades.

discolored sunset
peek through the clouds
grooming the wind
with earthly plaids.

we stand mute
our hands are freezing
the intensity of fall

settled on our shoes.

nostalgia is thick
the leaves are heaving
autumn is claiming
her fallen muse.

Midnight

The midnight reflects
a surreal cerulean shade
on the surface
of the calm silent lake.

The constellations
on the sky, quite visible
like scattered silver dust
on a pitch-black paper.

The fireflies with
their golden bulbs
light up the tree
near the cold waters.

Then crickets
gathered on a choir
to sing a late
night lullaby.

The shadow of the moon
is lost in the stray
of ash-colored cottons
in indefinite shapes.

The windswept pines
whisper through the wind...
calming the atmosphere
with a sweet nocturne.

The flowers are asleep
their petals, like heavy eyelids;
unaware of the
beauty of the night.

The gazebos are
unrestrained in silence
as darkness slowly
changes to a blue light.

Half the world is asleep
as I dream under the stars;
with a hefty heart
full of untold wishes.

And this magical beauty
which lays before my sight,
will be kept treasured
in an illusionist mind.

And as I drift
to a place called Neverland,
the night sky would sprinkle
golden dust from its wand.
And take me
where shattered hopes
wouldn't matter...
just dreams and things...

bizarre.

Paalam, tatay ko

my heart hangs askew
as the sky dissolves
in the mantle of his eyes

purple flowers
litter the scent
of a crumbling deathbed;
holy and organic,
like his temporal bones.

his sleeping face,
is an inkblot of a dying moth-
drawn to the light of vigil candles,
cradled by the psalms and prayers,
of his grieving church.

and i, his daughter,
sits on a polished pew,
steaming tears in absolute silence,

mumbling an incoherent goodbye.

The other side

i look for you
   between the slants
     of the pouring rain;
over and under
     the skin of the shapeless wind
         behind the veil
of drooping willows
   and dying tendrils
       of the setting sun.

       (but you are not here)

your eyes are shut
   from the clockwork
     of a finite life.
a forester drowning
     in a massive flood,
   brittle bones floating
       with the remains of
redwoods and pines.

   i still look for you
     in the crowd
   of graveyard flowers
       in the stillness

of a fading dawn
when lights are framed
    on stained glass windows

and hefty tears
        are yet to fall.

If i should go

if I should go
send me roses
and let them wither
on my palms.

crown me with
a circlet
crafted
with all shades of tulips.

lay me down
on a golden field
where the tendrils
of the sun
would reach me.

cover me
with a blooming blanket
of misty wildflowers
and
make me wear
my favorite yellow dress.

(please, please do not forget me)

i will be a butterfly
residing in the sky.
my silhouette is that
of the moving clouds;
my aureole-
the silver lining.

do not cry for me
for I will be home
if I should go.

Death hymn

I listen
to the spectral anthem
of thy soul-
like a stereo
set on Requiem.

Tear bags slit open,
droplets soak my cheeks.
Ivory skin shivers from the touch
of melancholy's paintbrush...
painting my heart blue.

Withered leaves
crunch under my wedges
like broken piano keys
on a forgotten recital.
The sky is groomed
with the darkest shade of gray
and the pines hum a sad song...
the wind never heard before.

I listen
to the spectral anthem
of thy soul...

As oscine singers
roost on brittle branches
swishing notes
from beaks to dewy breeze-
a sad song it is.

I listen
to the spectral anthem
of thy soul...

As the reaper
strums the broken strings
of thy heart-
percussion of a perishing dream-
grieving,
a departing melody...
a goodbye.

I listen
to the spectral anthem
of thy soul...
As I listen to the beat
of your heart...
no more.

Her second death

her soul
was a bird
roosting on brittle branches
of a dying tree.

one stone
from a slingshot
(like a catapult)
took her second life away.

the murderer-
a child of ten-
escaped the crime scene
with pride.

Repetition

this day is a repetition,
and i am old.
i have lived thousands of repetitions already.
i have witnessed
the rolling of the stars,
the aging of the sun,
the healing of the moon,
all these, and more;
nothing is different.

this day is a repetition,
a 24-hour cycle of hackneyed emotions-
of meeting and parting,
of having and losing,
of knowing and forgetting;
all these beginnings
and their trivial endings,
always recurring,
always the same;
nothing is different.

this day is a repetition
and i am lost counting.
i left my rationale in an old room
built yesterday.

i am aging.
i am obsolete.
i am an irony.
so are you.
we keep dusty days on repeat,
just where are we heading?

Introverted

she slipped from group hugs
like a midnight thief
and faded away
with the confused world.

she lost the smiles,
she lost the people,
she lost almost everything,

but that was the time,
she finally found

herself.

Talking to you is therapy

you listen to my ranting and musings,
whichever, and you smile with every pause i make.
i sound like a segmented poetry
on a parchment paper
interpreted by a two year old kid;
i am a walking confusion.
but i do not confuse you (hopefully).

i watch movies
with the least number of viewers.
i love the insignificant, the outcast, the unheard and
the never-seen-before.
i love old maps, old colors, wilting flowers,
and nostalgic tree houses.
i love scrapbooks and scrap papers.
i respect flaws the way you respect me.
i know i am a walking confusion
but i do not confuse you (hopefully).

bandwagon upsets me
and i can be too vulgar about it sometimes.
i carry a ton of quirks,
showing through my messy ways.
i am not a people person,
just imagine all the group hugs i missed.
i always get misunderstood.

but you always understand me.

just so you know,

talking to you is therapy.

Purple heart

love,

i fed you vignettes
and a spotless, blue sky.

why did you spit my heart
on the sidewalk?

Cosmic freckles

cosmic freckles
paint a sky of mauve blue,
sinking in a decoupage
of a velvet paper pulp,
sprawling shades of damp stars
on a whitewashed canvas.

he sits on a cinderblock moon,
tracing the edge of constellations,
watching the solar flares
dance on the surface
of his irises, as quasars
burn at his fragile touch.

Unloved

you have this bad habit
of scavenging for love;
carrying your bones around,
holding your hope
like a primary ticket
to a show
you know nothing about.

how lonely is that?

to hold the hands
that will soon let you go;
to play with words
you hardly even know

like: ***"I love you."***

Introspection

We are, each of us,
a set of temporal bones
made to last
for a lifetime (or less).

And we spend our sunrises
making connections and memories,
just so when the sunset comes
or when the crowd is gone,
we'll have something to accompany us
in our solitary moments-
when we are most vulnerable.

We sink on our beds
late at night
thinking about the people
who never think about us.

And we let movies and fiction
console our reality;
we are left dreaming
what is left to dream about,
only to wake up ascertaining none.

I am a face in the crowd, so are you.

We are fleeting memoirs.
We are numbers cast.
We are stories unheard.
We are personified emotions.

But in this world of good and bad,
love and ache,
smiles and frowns,
I would gladly hold
a memory of you.
Till I become
just a memory too.
And the crowd will remember us,
only to forget.

But loving you
is something
I would never regret.

The unread book

Creased pages cry silently,
Hardbound cover sneezes with dust,
The wonderful thoughts in inky prints,
Were all trapped in the past.

Cobwebs on the antique shelf,
Long for the touch of a feather duster,
And all the weary eyes skimmed through,
This retro-vintage wonder.

Fingers traced the old book's backbone;
Crisp and brown, wrinkled through time,
Forgotten by century-old souls,
Hoary sheets now bid goodbye.

This ancient piece breathes nostalgia,
A great story still concealed,
It begs for your attention,
'Read me please', the pages willed.

But words are mute, they can't persuade,
A voiceless tome with drowsy readers,
Some take a peek, then look away,
Leaving this treasure with no keepers.

So it waits, for years and years
Hoping eyes are never blinded
Forever stuck, filed on a ledge
Chapters bleed for reads (not) granted.

A poetess (5-7-5)

She bedaubed her heart
With gold glitters and dragees
To make it pretty.

She painted her lungs
A decoupage of petals:
Broken potpourri.

She dyed her marrows
The color of her lipstick:
Now she's bleeding pink.

Her soul, the rarest:
A multicolored patchwork
Of butterfly wings.

Her beautiful mind
wears a sweetbay magnolia
Like a laurel crown.

The flowers blossom
In the pit of her stomach
Never turning brown.

Her veins are silver

Sprawling on her pastel bones
Like glimmering vines.

Her skin, quite scented,
A wallpaper of roses
Made of pretty lines.

She is a poet.
Writer of immortal thoughts,
Guardian of her soul.

Her words resonate
Carried by the calmest wind
To his distant shore.

The fair lady

Woven butterflies on ascot so old,
Emblazoned on pastel fabric, so soft.
Worn by a blonde, hair dressed in chignon,
Stray curls hover in downright precision.

Emily Button, the lady so fair,
Iron-fresh frock, she so often wear.
Her eyes in blue sapphire resemble the sea,
A 'princess' she's called, all young gals envy.

Her plain petticoat in beige was the best,
Coated in a ruffled fruity pink dress.
Her lips, cherry-colored; her skin's ivory.
She has rose-tinted cheeks, pure femininity.

And in golden light, she's out of her cage;
Of gold pillars and stones, brass in old age.
She'll paint her garden in emerald hues,
Bathed in sunshine and a palette of dews.

And in the gazebo, she'll drink her tea,
A scene highlighted by a sycamore tree.
Her life is a dream designed to be real.
Crafted perfection, truly surreal.

Bulaklak sa parang

Ikaw ay bulaklak sa parang ng buhay-
Nakatunghay sa isang masalimuot na mundo.
Nakagapos sa lupa ang iyong mga paa,
Kapalad ng mga ligaw na damo.

Sikapin mong ngitian ang araw at mga bituin-
Damhin mo ang maginhawang ihip ng hangin.
Dumaan man ang mga unos at bagyo,
Subukan mo sanang sumibol ng buo.

Ikaw ay bulaklak sa parang ng buhay,
Sadyang marikit, mahalimuyak at makulay.
Ngunit balang araw, kariktan mo'y mawawala,
Babalik ka sa lupa, kung saan ka nagmula.

Mga dahon mo'y malalagas sa paglaon.
Mga talulot mo'y lilipasan ng panahon.
Gagapasin ang mga damo, ikaw ay matitira.
Mamumulaklak ng mabini, para lamang malanta.

Ikaw ay bulaklak sa parang ng buhay...

Takipsilim

sa pag-ihip ng hangin
nabuhag ang tumpok
ng mga tuyong dahon,
nagsisayaw sa saliw
ng musikang kay lumbay,
umikot, pumataas,
upang muling sumayad
sa uhaw na lupa.

ang mga puno ay nakayuko,
nakikidalamhati
sa mga ulap na kulay abo,
humalukipkip sa lamig,
pinaghahandaan ang
nagbabadyang ulan
habang nakatitig ng diretso
sa masaganang kawalan.

sa di kalayuan,
dalawang anino ang nakatayo;
kapwa nagpapahid ng
kanya-kanyang mga luha.
pumagitna ang katahimikan,
pumainlang ang lungkot,
at sa tagpong iyon,

isang puso ang nadurog.

nalusaw ang mga imahe
sa pagbabaliktanaw.
ilang taon na ang lumipas,
pero randam pa rin ang ginaw.
bumagal ang takbo ng mundo,
animo ay napagod.
sa walang hanggang pag-ibig,
sadyang di tayo umabot.

About the Author

Icy Belen Tumayao is a twenty-six-year-old writer from Tigbauan, Iloilo, Philippines. She is passionate about art, and all its mediums and derivatives; and wanted to share her contribution through poetry. She is unfathomably in love with words, and with all the tender details comprising literature. Her poetry focuses on the human condition, the tangled threads of connectivity bridging one soul to another. Most of her works are narratives of reimagined realities; with all the encounters and departures, and everything in between. She explores the skewness of love and the vulnerability of the human spirit, in all its shames and glories, to seek a deeper understanding of the world. Charles Bukowski is her greatest poetic inspiration.

www.ingramcontent.com/pod-product-compliance
Lightning Source LLC
LaVergne TN
LVHW091710190726
843493LV00001B/237